The MAJIK
Gopher

Written by Christopher R. Swanson

Foreword by Robert R. Swanson (MY DAD)

Illustrations by Susan Krupp

Created by AuthorSource Media
Edited by Simon Presland

This timeless book is dedicated to the man who always put his family ahead of himself ... my dad, the original Majik Gopher.

Foreword by Robert R. Swanson

In the early 1970s, while employed for a national sales organization, I was required to travel out of state for business. With four rambunctious youngsters to take care of, I'm grateful that my wife, Grace Ann, was a stay-at-home mom.

At the end of each business day, I missed my family and would look forward to my call home. My wife always had the children take turns talking to Dad. One day, after my daily call ended, I decided to send each of my children a personally addressed note in the mail. They loved receiving their own mail! Later, I decided to bring home a small gift, but I wanted to make it a surprise. My idea was to package the gift in a brown lunch bag, put some paw prints on the outside of the bag, and write a message that the gift was from "The Majik Gopher." My reason: The children received gifts from Santa, the Easter Bunny and the Tooth Fairy, so they needed a fictional character to justify a gift for no occasion, other than they were sad—and so was Dad—that I was not home. Good enough for me!

My plan worked.

Before I would leave on a trip, the kids would ask if The Majik Gopher would bring a gift. Then their mother and I had another idea. When any of the kids were ill, or if there was some other event that caused them to be sad—such as having to move to another state because I received a business promotion, or one of their friends had moved—The Majik Gopher would pay a visit. It didn't take long for our children to catch on. We obliged and the whole idea took off! Most often when The Majik Gopher visited, each child would get a note with their gift. Sometimes he would put a gift in a special place without a note— like my briefcase or a bag in the house—which would surprise us all.

When our children reached adulthood and married, they continued this tradition with their children. And my grandchildren ask me if The Majik Gopher was going to visit whenever they were injured or ill. We now have a third generation enjoying The Majik Gopher fable.

I invite you to make MG part of your family!

All the best,

Robert R. Swanson

In a prairie field far away lives a family of loveable, huggable gophers.

Mama gopher picks big bright berries while Daddy gopher works in the field.

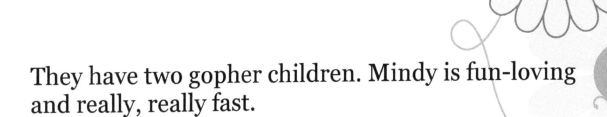

They have two gopher children. Mindy is fun-loving and really, really fast.

She's always scurrying around the house or racing her friends up and down hills.

Mindy is pretty and always seems to do everything right.

Mindy has a little brother. His name is Majik.

Majik is not very fast at all. He runs and runs but can never keep up with the other gophers.

Majik was born with tiny paws. Too tiny to run and too tiny to dig. Too tiny to pick berries and too tiny to work.

Majik doesn't have many gopher friends; they won't come to play because he's different.

This makes Majik very sad.

But Majik has a special gift that no other gopher has.

Majik can hear the tiniest sounds no one else can.

Like the whispering of baby mice, the swishing wings of a new butterfly, and the falling tears of sad children around the world.

This is what makes Majik so special. He listens ... and he uses his special gift to help others.

He helps sick people in the hospital. Children hurt from falling off their bike. Majik even helps big people who don't feel anyone loves them or hears them!

In fact, Majik can make *anyone* feel loved and important!

How, you ask?

When Majik finds someone in need, and they are fast asleep or when they look away for a split second, he sneaks in their favorite candy or a brand-new toy. He leaves it in a special place like under their pillow, at the end of their bed, or even at the doorstep.

Children of all ages and all over the world love The MAJIK Gopher—because he listens to them and most important of all, he shows them how much he cares.

Majik loves people others don't and loves them when others won't.

He also leaves a little note like this one ...

Here's how you can be like MAJIK:

When you know someone is sick, sad or hurt, or maybe they just don't feel important, you can leave a special treat along with a note signed, The Majik Gopher.

Just by listening to people and showing them they are loved, you can make the world feel better and special again—and that's the MAJIK that makes the difference!

What's Your Special Gift?

ABOUT THE AUTHOR

Christopher R. Swanson is a 4-time IRONMAN
finisher, two-time author, inspirational speaker,
and CEO of Swanson Leadership. He is the
Sheriff of Genesee County, Flint, Michigan.
Chris's influence has been felt around the world.
He is married to Jamie, and they have two sons,
Riley and Jordan.

CPSIA information can be obtained
at www.ICGtesting.com
Printed in the USA
LVHW071600131220
674080LV00049B/3247